⭐ Contents ⭐

Giddy-Up
Ghost Town

by Rebecca Gómez

Disney
PRESS

New York

Printed in the United States of America

First Edition
1 3 5 7 9 10 8 6 4 2

Library of Congress Catalog Card Number: 00-101751

ISBN 0-7868-4443-4

For more Disney Press fun, visit www.disneybooks.com

1. Creepy Camp-out

It was a dark, quiet night. Bright stars twinkled in the inky black sky. Woody, the Prospector, Jessie, and Bullseye sprawled around a small, bright campfire. The Prospector had just come back from Bubbling Creek, where he'd washed up their supper dishes.

The Roundup gang was mighty tired after their busy day—they had just captured the worst chicken thief in Dry Gulch County and put him behind bars. Still, they weren't quite ready to

head back into Dry Gulch just yet. They liked to be together in the great outdoors.

"Who's ready for some popcorn?" cried Woody.

"I am!" said both Jessie and the Prospector. Bullseye just whinnied.

"Well, Jessie," Woody said, "I'll whip us up some popcorn, if you'll agree to tell us some of your ghost stories."

"It's a deal," said Jessie.

Woody grinned, because he loved Jessie's

ghost stories. Even though he'd heard them many, many times, they still gave him goose bumps and made him look over his shoulder at the slightest noise.

The Prospector looked nervous. Sometimes he found Jessie's stories a little bit too scary.

"Tell us the story about the legendary peg-legged pirate of Dry Gulch!" Woody said as he settled down with his popcorn.

The Prospector shivered at the thought of the peg-legged pirate. He had lived in a cave near Dry Gulch about a hundred years ago. Legend had it that the pirate's wicked eyes could still be seen glowing in the dark of night whenever his spirit got angry. The Prospector sure didn't want to hear Jessie tell *that* story again.

"Bullseye's lookin' mighty thirsty," the Prospector said. "I'll take this poor varmint down to the creek to get a drink."

And so the Prospector and Bullseye wandered down to the creek for a big gulp of water. It was a calm night, but the crickets were singing loudly. The Prospector could see a few lights burning brightly in Dry Gulch, on the far side of

Bubbling Creek. Everything looked quiet in the sleepy town.

Bullseye drank his fill of cool water, then started back toward the campfire. The Prospector followed him. "I wish Jessie would tell a funny story once in a while!" he whispered to the horse.

Just as they were climbing the ridge to their

campfire, the Prospector heard a strange noise.
Something was creaking and clanging. The
noise was coming from Dry Gulch! The
Prospector glanced over at his friends to see if
they had heard the noise too. Jessie was on her
feet, waving her arms and making scary faces.
Woody was wide-eyed with fright—and so
engrossed in Jessie's yarn that he wouldn't have
heard a whole herd of buffalo go stampeding by!

The Prospector really didn't want to hear the
gruesome end to the creepy ghost story. Then,

once again, he heard that strange noise coming from Dry Gulch.

"What in tarnation was that?!" cried the Prospector. He shook his head. "I've got to find out what it is."

And so the Prospector climbed onto Bullseye's back and the two headed back over the ridge toward Dry Gulch.

2. The Ghouliest Gulch in the Wild, Wild West

As he and Bullseye splashed through the cool water of the creek, the Prospector kept his eyes on Dry Gulch. All appeared calm and quiet. But the quiet was interrupted every few minutes by that strange creaking and clanging sound.

"What on earth could be making that noise?" the Prospector wondered out loud. "As a sworn member of the Roundup gang, it's my duty to help keep the peace out here in the Wild West. I'd better go investigate and make sure that nobody's in trouble! Giddy-up, Bullseye!"

The Prospector was a little uncertain of what

he would do if he actually saw somebody in trouble. After all, he usually tracked down thieves and troublemakers with Woody, Jessie, and Bullseye as a team. But he felt pretty sure that he could stop a lawbreaker by himself. If worse came to worst, he could just run back to the campfire and get the rest of the Roundup gang.

"Besides," he told himself, "that creaking noise is probably nothing at all. Maybe somebody just left their barn door open, and it's swinging back and forth in the wind."

Except, he realized, there wasn't any wind! Not even a whisper of a breeze stirred in Bullseye's mane or pushed the tumbleweeds that were scattered on the ground.

The Prospector shivered. He tried not to let himself get spooked. He just concentrated on the funny noise and made his way into Dry Gulch.

Just as it had appeared from the opposite side

of the creek, all was quiet in the frontier town. There wasn't a single person out on the streets. The general store was completely dark, but the Prospector could see lights shining from the windows of some of the houses he passed. Every once in a while, he caught a glimpse of a shadow moving behind curtained windows.

"Everything seems okay, but it's a little bit too

quiet for my likin'," the Prospector said to himself. He jumped down and peered into the darkness.

Just then, the Prospector noticed something odd. What were those strange lights glowing behind the general store?

The Prospector gulped. It could be only one thing—the glowing eyes of the peg-legged pirate!

3. Shhhhhhh!

The Prospector stared straight ahead, his knees knocking together. Bullseye looked up and saw the strange shapes, too. Before he could stop himself, he gave a frightened "Neigh!"

Like every gold-digger worth his weight in shiny rocks, the Prospector was terrified of the peg-legged pirate. He had heard one too many of Jessie's scary stories! Still, he decided that he had to go and investigate. It was his duty as a member of the Roundup gang!

So, climbing up onto Bullseye's back, the

Prospector moved closer and closer to the weird, glowing lights.

Suddenly, the Prospector realized that the creaking and clanging noises had stopped. It was way too quiet!

Just as he passed the sheriff's office (boy, how he wished Woody was sitting inside!), the Prospector heard what sounded like shuffling feet behind him. He stopped Bullseye and slid off his back, goose bumps rising up on his arms. But suddenly, the noises stopped. Terrified of what he might see, the Prospector took his eyes off the glowing lights and looked back over his shoulder. Bullseye looked too.

Nothing! There was no one behind them!

Bullseye gave himself a good shake and a snort. "I know, I know," the Prospector whispered. "We must be imagining things. Let's just

focus on the peg-legged pirate. One thing at a time!"

But when the Prospector looked up, he couldn't believe his eyes. The glowing eyes had disappeared! Just then, the shuffling noises sounded again behind him! This time, they were joined by a clanking noise.

Bullseye whirled around in a circle. The street behind them was dark and empty.

"I'd know that sound anywhere," the

Prospector said. "That's the sound that spurs make! Spurs! Now, who'd be sneaking around Dry Gulch at night wearing spurs?"

The Prospector could come up with only one answer to that question: *horse thieves!*

4. Pirates and Horse Thieves and Ghosts

"**T**hieves!" the Prospector whispered to Bullseye. The Prospector didn't know what to do, and he was too frightened to think clearly. "And to think I thought listening to one of Jessie's stories was scary!" he said.

"Okay, Bullseye," he said to the petrified horse. "Get ahold of yourself. What would Woody and Jessie do?"

That was easy to figure out: Woody and Jessie would come up with a great plan to catch the bad guys. Then they would ride, whoopin' and

hollerin' through the streets, scaring any thieves half to death.

But what could he and Bullseye, all alone, hope to do?

Telling himself to be brave, the Prospector forced himself to walk slowly down the street, searching for the source of the noise.

That's when the Prospector saw something that made his blood run cold, and his hair stand

on end. Big white shapes were gliding silently down the street not a stone's throw away from him.

"Ghosts!" the Prospector screamed. "I'll stay here and protect the town while you go get help! Run like the wind, Bullseye!"

Bullseye reared up. With a loud whinny, he turned on his hooves and dashed out of Dry

Gulch. Running like the peg-legged pirate himself was after him, Bullseye splashed back across the creek and made a beeline for Woody and Jessie, still sitting at the campfire. The Prospector was left shiverin' scared in the middle of town.

Woody and Jessie looked up in surprise when Bullseye came snorting and galloping up to the campfire.

"Whoa, there, big fella!" cried Jessie. "You 'bout scared me half to death!"

"What's got you so excited, Bullseye?" Woody asked. "You look like you've seen a ghost!"

Bullseye snorted and pawed the ground. Woody and Jessie could tell he needed help from his friends and he needed it fast!

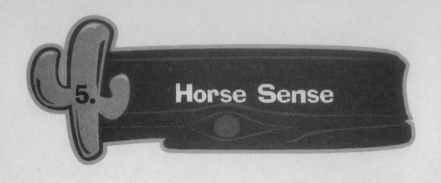

5. Horse Sense

"**B**ullseye, what's wrong?" asked Jessie. "You really look frightened. Where is the Prospector?"

Bullseye snorted and shook his head again.

"You know," said Woody, "it seems that Bullseye is trying to tell us something. Let's see if we can figure out what it is.

"First off," Woody started, "where were you?"

Bullseye pranced over to the edge of the ridge and shook his head toward Dry Gulch.

"I've got this one," shouted Jessie. "I speak horse! Bullseye's telling us he was in Dry Gulch!"

"Aw, Jessie," Woody answered, "that was eas-
ier than roping a sleeping calf!"

"What happened in Dry Gulch?" asked Jessie.

Bullseye stepped closer to the campfire, and
his horseshoe accidentally clanked against the
Prospector's gold pan. "Milk bottles!" Woody
yelled.

"No, your *horseshoes* are achin', right
Bullseye?" Jessie chimed in.

"Horseshoes? He's obviously saying the Prospector found some gold in the creek," Woody insisted.

"That doesn't sound like gold," Jessie argued. "Bullseye is sayin' he feels like dancin'."

Woody and Jessie guessed and guessed, but they didn't even come close.

"Wild turkeys!" cried Jessie finally. "I think Bullseye saw wild turkeys over near Dry Gulch and decided to chase one."

Jessie was sure she was right, and soon convinced Woody that Bullseye really was trying to say "wild turkeys."

Next, Bullseye scooted up close to the fire and knelt down. He wasn't trying to tell Woody and Jessie anything, he was just trying to find a safe place far away from the glowing eyes of the peg-legged pirate.

"Snakes!" shouted Woody when he saw Bullseye kneeling close to the ground. "Bullseye saw snakes in Dry Gulch! Bullseye hates snakes, that's probably why he ran back here so quickly!"

This time, Woody was so sure that he was right that soon Jessie was agreeing with him.

Bullseye stood up and moved even closer to the campfire.

"I've got it!" cried Jessie. "Bullseye tried to put out a brushfire in Dry Gulch. Bullseye knows how dangerous brushfires are; that's why he came back to get our help!"

Poor Bullseye! He knew he had to get back to Dry Gulch to the Prospector. He had no idea why Woody and Jessie kept talking to him instead of coming with him back into town. He opened his eyes wide and nickered softly to try to get their attention.

"Baby woodland critters!" hollered Jessie. "Bullseye saw some baby woodland critters and came to get us to help them. Oh, Bullseye, you're the best!" With that, Jessie gave Bullseye a big hug and rubbed his nose.

Bullseye pulled himself away from Jessie and

started back toward Dry Gulch. Whether or not the rest of the gang knew it, something was wrong in that town, and they needed to go find the Prospector and investigate!

"Okay, Bullseye," Woody said. "We'll come with you. We'll find the Prospector and chase the snakes and wild turkeys who attacked him and put out the brushfire and rescue the little woodland critters!"

"Good thing we understand Bullseye so well," Jessie said, grabbing a lantern. She and Woody hopped onto Bullseye's back and made their way across the creek and toward Dry Gulch.

6. The Roundup Gang to the Rescue

"**W**e should sneak into town slowly," Woody advised. "After all, we don't want to scare those wild turkeys."

"But let's hurry, Woody," said Jessie. "I want to help those poor, helpless woodland critters."

As they made their way quietly into town, Woody and Jessie heard the creaking and clanging noise that had first drawn the Prospector and Bullseye to Dry Gulch.

When the noise stopped, a voice came out of the darkness.

"Who goes there?" the voice said.

Woody, Jessie, and Bullseye jumped with a start. "We come in peace," Woody said, raising the lantern to see who it was.

"Well I'll be hog-tied and dipped in pancake batter—it's you!" the Prospector said, stepping out from the shadows.

"Prospector," said Woody, "Bullseye says he saw some wild turkeys."

"I don't know about turkeys," the Prospector

said. "But explain *that!*" The Prospector pointed into the distance. There they were again! The strange glowing eyes he and Bullseye had seen! Bullseye gave Jessie a nudge with his nose.

Jessie followed the Prospector's gaze. "The peg-legged pirate!" she whispered.

"Okay," said Woody, trying to sound brave. "Let's stay calm. I'm going to sneak up for a closer look."

He crept quietly through some bushes, Jessie

close behind him. Woody held his breath. Could it really be the ghost of the peg-legged pirate? Suddenly he gasped. "Those aren't the pirate's eyes!" he cried. "They're lanterns!"

"Well I'll be!" said Jessie. "I believe you're right!"

And it was true—the spooky floating eyes were nothing but a bunch of lanterns dangling from some trees!

The Prospector felt a little sheepish, but then he remembered about the thieves and the ghosts. Just let Woody find a funny explanation for them!

"**W**ell, that's one mystery solved," said Woody. "But who hung up these lanterns?"

"Yes, and what about the brushfire and the baby woodland critters?" asked Jessie.

"Don't worry, Jessie," Woody answered. "If anyone or anything around here needs help, we're around to provide it."

"Prospector, where did you see the brushfire?" asked Woody.

"Brushfire? There wasn't any brushfire!" the Prospector insisted. "Why'd you tell 'em that, you

silly horse? Sure as day, there were thieves sneaking around Dry Gulch!"

The Prospector shook his head and started in the direction of the sheriff's building. Maybe they'd see the horse thieves on their way.

So the Roundup gang followed the Prospector. As they got close to the sheriff's office, there was a faint shuffling and jingling sound.

Bullseye's ears pricked up. "Bullseye hears something!" cried Jessie.

"Shhh!" said the Prospector. "We'll never

catch the thieves with you hollering like that!"

The whole gang stood stock-still and listened.

"Why, that sounds like people walking," said Woody. "And the sound is coming from the other side of my office. Let's go look!"

The Roundup gang rushed toward the back of the sheriff's office and saw a whole crowd of townspeople going for a walk. They smiled and said "hello" to the Roundup gang. They were dressed up very nicely, and many of them were carrying bulging sacks.

"Evening, ma'am. What's going on?" Woody

asked a woman as she walked by.

"Oh, nothing, Sheriff," she answered politely. "We're all just trying to get a bit of exercise and fresh air."

"Exercise!" cried Jessie. "But it's nighttime, and you're all dressed up!"

The woman just smiled and waved as she walked past them.

Woody shook his head. "Come on, let's go inside the office and try to put this whole thing together."

Bullseye stayed outside while the three trooped into Woody's office. Jessie plopped right down in a chair. "Why, I don't think Bullseye was saying 'brushfire' at all," said Jessie. "I think he was saying 'crazy people'!"

"Now, Jessie," said Woody, "if the people of Dry Gulch choose to dress up and go out in the moonlight to get a bit of fresh air, then that's their business."

"Okay, fine," answered Jessie. "But Woody, what about the woodland critters?"

"Ah, yes. The woodland critters," said Woody.

"I wonder how we misunderstood Bullseye with that one?"

"Woodland critters?" the Prospector said, straightening out his hat and shooting Woody a funny look.

8. A Shocking Surprise . . .

A whole half hour had gone by and the Roundup gang was no closer to finding an explanation for the strange events of the evening. The Prospector still felt a little sheepish, seeing as how the eyes of the peg-legged pirate had turned out to be lanterns, and the supposed horse thieves were really just townspeople out for a moonlight stroll.

But the Prospector was sure that he'd seen ghosts. What else could explain the shivery white shapes?

"All right, Prospector," Jessie said, "where did

you see those baby woodland critters?"

"For heck's sake, there weren't any woodland critters!" the Prospector said, fuming mad. "What are you listenin' to a horse for? If I say we saw ghosts, then we saw *ghosts*, and you gotta believe me!"

The Prospector stormed out of the sheriff's office, Woody and Jessie right behind him. "I'm going to get to the bottom of this," he said, and led the gang toward the general store, where he'd seen the ghosts last.

"We don't want to scare the critters," said Jessie. "So let's be very quiet."

"Good thinking, Jessie," said Woody. "Except I thought we were looking for ghosts."

"Ghosts, woodland critters, flyin' gorillas— either way ya better be quiet or you'll scare them away!" the Prospector whispered.

Walking closely together, the gang made their way silently around to the back of the general store. As they slowly turned the corner into the backyard, they heard

"SURPRISE!"

There, spread out in front of them, was a huge party. All the townspeople had gathered for a celebration. There were long tables set up, with lots of cookies and cakes and ice cream on them. There was another table piled with brightly wrapped gifts. Bullseye noticed that there were several bales of sweet-smelling hay just for him. There were lanterns tied to tree branches. And, best of all, there was a giant banner draped between trees, which said:

THE CITIZENS OF DRY GULCH
SALUTE THE ROUNDUP GANG!

"A party?" cried Woody.

"A surprise party for you!" answered one of the townsfolk. "I thought you'd figure things out when you walked in on me hanging up the lanterns. I had to hide behind a tree!"

"Three cheers for Sheriff Woody and the Roundup gang!" cried someone else.

As the whole crowd cheered, the Prospector

scratched his head. He had an explanation for the strange noises, the spooky floating eyes, and the horse thieves, but what about the ghosts? Then he noticed that the tables were covered with crisp white cloths. He must have seen sneaky party-goers carrying the tablecloths!

"All in all, it's been a mixed-up night," said Woody.

"Yes, but this is the rootin' tootin'est party I've ever seen!" cried Jessie. "And it's in our honor! Yee-hah!"

"Thanks for getting the gang to come to my rescue, Bullseye!" said the Prospector, giving the horse a big hug. Jessie and Woody joined him.

"I'm glad there weren't any pirates or ghosts or horse thieves," said Woody. "It just goes to show you. You can't believe everything you see—or *think* you see!"

Jessie threw her hat up into the air. "Giddy-up ghost town, let's have us some fun!"

WOODY'S ROUNDUP

It's
Rodeo time
in **Dry Gulch**

Jessie is going head to head with Big John, the meanest cowpoke in the West. They are neck and neck when it comes to ropin' calves, ridin' bulls, and racin' horses. But will Jessie's chances of winning the rodeo title be ruined by Big John?

Is Big John playin' fair?

Find out in Woody's Roundup #3:
Ride 'Em Rodeo!

SEPTEMBER 2000

Look for these exciting titles from DISNEY INTERACTIVE

Catch the learning buzz with Disney's Buzz Lightyear Learning Series.